HECTOR PROTECTOR
AND
AS I WENT OVER THE WATER

HECTOR PROTECTOR
AND
AS I WENT OVER THE WATER

TWO NURSERY RHYMES WITH PICTURES
BY
MAURICE SENDAK

PictureLions
An Imprint of HarperCollinsPublishers

First published in the USA by Harper & Row, 1965
First published in Great Britain by The Bodley Head Children's Books, 1967

Published in Picture Lions 1992
Picture Lions is an imprint of the Children's Division,
part of HarperCollins Publishers Limited,
77-85 Fulham Palace Road, Hammersmith,
London W6 8JB

Printed in Hong Kong

Hector Protector was dressed all in green.

Hector Protector was sent to the queen.

The queen did not like him

no more did the king

so Hector Protector was sent back again.

AS I WENT OVER THE WATER

FOR BARBARA

As I went over the water

the water went over me.

I saw two little blackbirds sitting on a tree.

One called me a rascal

and one called me a thief.

I took up my little black stick

and knocked out all their teeth !